Do you remember the little piggy who went to market?
Did someone wiggle your toes and tickle you as the little pig ran
wee wee wee all the way home? Well, *This Little Piggy Went Singing*
was inspired by the traditional rhyme:

This little piggy went to market
This little piggy stayed home
This little piggy had roast beef
This little piggy had none
And this little piggy went wee wee wee all the way home.

This Little Piggy Went Singing

This Little Piggy

Went Singing

Margaret Wild *and* Deborah Niland

ALLEN&UNWIN

SYDNEY • MELBOURNE • AUCKLAND • LONDON

This little piggy
stayed home

This little piggy
went singing

This little piggy
had noodles

And this little piggy went

toot, toot, toot

This little piggy
had none

all the way home.

This little piggy
went shopping

This little piggy
stayed home

This little piggy
had meatballs

And this little piggy went

vroom, vroom, vroom

This little piggy
had none

all the way home.

This little piggy
went posting

This little piggy
stayed home

This little piggy
had berries

This little piggy
had none

And this little piggy went

plink, plonk, plonk

all the way home.

This little piggy
went dining

This little piggy
had candy canes

This little piggy
stayed home

And this little piggy went

ratta-
tat-
tat

This little piggy
had none

all the way home.

This little piggy
went partying

This little piggy
had watermelon

This little piggy
stayed home

And this little piggy went

jingle-jingle-jingle

This little piggy
had none

all the way home.

This little piggy
stayed home

This little piggy
had plum pudding

This little piggy
went riding

This little piggy
had none

And this little piggy went

tra, la, la

all the way home.

This little piggy
went dancing

This little piggy
stayed home

This little piggy
had pineapple

And this little piggy went

tweet, tweet, tweet

This little piggy
had none

all the way home.

This little piggy
went visiting

This little piggy
had milkshake

This little piggy
stayed home

And this little piggy went

ringa-ding-ding

all the way home.

This little piggy
had none

This little piggy
went star-gazing

This little piggy
stayed home

This little piggy
had gingerbread

This little piggy
had none

And this little piggy went

ho, ho, ho, ho, ho

all the way home!

Margaret Wild is one of Australia's most highly respected authors of books for young people. She has published over seventy picture books for young children, including *On the Day You Were Born*, *The Dream of the Thylacine*, *Fox*, *Rosie and Tortoise* and *Old Pig* (all with Ron Brooks), *Ruby Roars* (with Kerry Argent), *The Treasure Box* (with Freya Blackwood) and *Tanglewood* (with Vivienne Goodman). Her other books with Deborah Niland are *Chatterbox* and *Grandpa Baby*.

Margaret has been the recipient of the Nan Chauncy Award and the Lady Culter Award for her contributions to Australian children's literature.

Deborah Niland is an artist and illustrator who has created many of her own picture books, including *It's Bedtime William*, *Annie's Chair*, *Annie to the Rescue* and *Double Trouble*. She has illustrated many other books, too, including *The Tall Man and the Twelve Babies* (with Tom Niland Champion and Kilmeny Niland), the classic *Mulga Bill's Bicycle*, *When the Wind Changed* and *There's a Hippopotamus on Our Roof Eating Cake*.

www.deborah-niland.com.au

First published in 2014

Allen & Unwin
83 Alexander Street
Crows Nest NSW 2065
Australia
Phone: (61 2) 8425 0100
Email: info@allenandunwin.com
Web: www.allenandunwin.com

A Cataloguing-in-Publication entry is available from the National Library of Australia
www.trove.nla.gov.au

ISBN 978 174331 912 3

Cover and text design by Sandra Nobes
Set in 20 pt ITC Century Light by Sandra Nobes
Prepress by Megan Ellis
This book was printed in July 2014 at Hang Tai Printing (Guang Dong) Ltd., Xin Cheng Ind Est, Xie Gang Town, Dong Guan, Guang Dong Province, China.

10 9 8 7 6 5 4 3 2 1